Harry and Toto

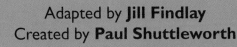

Empty and Full

For Ella

Adapted by **Jill Findlay**
Created by **Paul Shuttleworth**

Based on the TV series Harry and Toto
and the TV Script "Empty and Full" written by Myles McLeod
performed by Bob Golding and Sue Devaney
with the music of Liz Kitchen

Original design by
Marcin Wasilewski
Robert Jaszczurowski
Łukasz Kacprowicz

Additional design and book layout by
SunHouse Creative

With special thanks to Loretta Cocchi, Nigel Gamble and BBC Worldwide
together with Chris Rose, Kay Benbow, Michael Carrington
and everyone at BBC Children's

It's breakfast time in Opposite Town, the most important meal of the day.

Everyone is filling their empty tummies before heading off for a busy day at work.

Gillie the Giraffe is in charge of Opposite Stores.

She fills up the empty
shelves in the food department.

Eric the Elephant is the town's firefighter.

He makes sure his fire engine is full of water.

Horace the Horse is emptying the post box.

It's full of letters for him to deliver.

"It's going to be a busy day," says Horace. "I'm glad I had a big breakfast."

Toto the Tortoise has
just had breakfast too.

"I'm full," he says.

He's about to wash up when...

Ring, ring!

The telephone rings.

It's Toto's best friend, Harry the Hare.

"Would you like to come over for something to eat?" asks Harry.

"That's kind," says Toto, "but I'm full to the brim with breakfast."

"But Toto, you walk so slowly that by the time you get here, it'll be lunchtime!"

"You're right!" says Toto.
"I'll leave now."

"Hmm," wonders Harry, "where did I put my recipe book?"

Harry can't find it, so he empties everything out of his kitchen cupboards.

"At last! There it is."

Harry and Toto live at opposite ends of Opposite Town, so it takes Toto all morning to reach Harry's house.

Toto is so hungry, he can't wait to see what Harry is making for lunch.

"What's on the menu Harry?"
asks Toto.

"I don't know," replies Harry, "I've spent all morning looking for the recipe book! I'm sure there'll be something in the fridge."

Open the fridge door and see what's inside...

...one green pea.

"It's empty!" cries Harry.

Harry the Hare has a problem.
Now it's your turn to help him.

Harry needs to get some food for lunch.
Who do you think can help?

Is it Horace the Horse,
Eric the Elephant
or Gillie the Giraffe?

Who sells food in Opposite Stores?

It's Gillie the Giraffe.

"Can I help you?" asks Gillie.

Toto asks Gillie to fill
a carton with olives.
"Of course," says Gillie,
"big or small?"

Toto likes to take his time
choosing his favourites.

Harry likes to speed round
the shop. The trolley gets full
very quickly.

"I'm the fastest shopper in
Opposite Town," he laughs.

"That was quick," says Toto.
"Let's go-go-go-go to the
    checkout," says Harry.

"Harry has invited me to his house for lunch," Toto tells Gillie.

"Well the food looks delicious," replies Gillie, "some of my favourites, in fact. Do you need help packing it?"

"It's okay, I can do it myself," replies Harry as he fills the bag.

"Do you need help eating it?" offers Gillie.

"We can do that ourselves too," laughs Harry. "Ooh this is going to be the best lunch ever."

"Be careful Harry," warns Toto. "Make sure the bag isn't too full or it might break."

"Enjoy your lunch," says Gillie as she waves goodbye.

Harry picks up the shopping bag but doesn't notice when it breaks.

He leaves all the food behind him. Silly Harry!

"It's very light," Harry tells his friend.
"Why isn't it heavy any more?"

Do you know?

Back at Harry's house, Toto looks inside the bag.

"Hang on," he says.

"It's **empty** and it should be **full.**"

"Where's the shopping?" says a puzzled Harry.

Toto is wondering if he will ever get his lunch when suddenly, the doorbell rings.

It's Gillie the Giraffe with Harry and Toto's shopping!

"Gillie, you've saved the day," laughs Toto. "Thanks to you, our tummies won't be empty."

Suddenly, there is a funny loud noise.

Rumble! Rumble!

What do you think it could be?

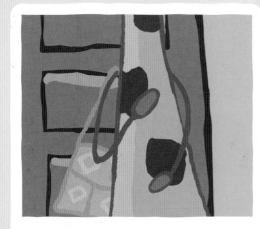

"Oh Gillie," giggles Harry, "it sounds as if your tummy is empty too."

"Yes, I haven't had *my* lunch yet," hints Gillie.

Harry invites Gillie to have lunch with him and Toto.

"Oh, thank you," says Gillie, "I thought you'd never ask!"

Harry and Toto are always finding opposites. If you enjoyed reading Empty and Full then look out for the other Opposite Stories.

Stop and **Go**
Created by Paul Shuttleworth

Quiet and **Loud**
Created by Paul Shuttleworth

Land and **Sea**
Created by Paul Shuttleworth